THE BIG
ALFIE
OUT OF DOORS
STORYBOOK

Text copyright © 1992 by Shirley Hughes
First published in Great Britain by The Bodley Head
All rights reserved. No part of this book may be reproduced or utilized in any form or by any means, electronic
or mechanical, including photocopying and recording, or by any information storage and retrieval system,
without permission in writing from the Publisher. Inquiries should be addressed to Lothrop, Lee & Shepard Books,
a division of William Morrow & Company, Inc., 1350 Avenue of the Americas, New York, New York 10019.
Printed in Hong Kong.

First U.S. Edition 1 2 3 4 5 6 7 8 9 10
Library of Congress Cataloging in Publication Data
Hughes, Shirley. The big Alfie out of doors storybook / by Shirley Hughes.   p.   cm.   Summary: Preschooler
Alfie has pleasant outdoor adventures with various family members, including his sister Annie Rose, Grandma,
and Dad.   ISBN 0-688-11428-8   [1. Family life—Fiction.]   I. Title.   PZ7.H87395Bj   1992   [E]—dc20
91-28635 CIP AC

SHIRLEY HUGHES
THE BIG
ALFIE
OUT OF DOORS
STORYBOOK

Lothrop Lee & Shepard Books   New York

Shop

In Alfie's backyard there was a big bush. You could lift up a curtain of leaves and walk inside. It was a nice private place.

One afternoon Mom gave Alfie a long cardboard box to play with. He took it into the bush and put it down on its side. It made a good counter for a shop.

Then Alfie and Annie Rose looked around the yard for something to sell in the shop. They found plenty of things lying about: flower petals, seed pods, acorn cups, and lots of different kinds of leaves. They laid them out on the counter, using some very big leaves as plates.

They pretended they had vegetables and potato chips and sweets and ice creams in their shop (not the kind you can really eat, of course), and toys, too. When everything was nicely arranged, Alfie decided that what the shop needed now was some money. He fetched a little brown box with a lid, and they collected a lot of flat greenish-yellow seeds which rattled about inside like real money.

Mom and Grandma were sitting in the yard having a cup of tea. Alfie asked them if they were coming to buy something at the shop.

"Yes, of course," said Grandma, "but what's the name of your shop? Is it the Alfie and Annie Rose General Store?"

"No," said Alfie. "It's called Lewis Burrows and Company." He knew that there was a proper shop called that in the High Street.

Alfie put on his peaked cap to open up the shop, and Annie Rose wore an apron to be Mr. Lewis Burrows' lady assistant.

Then Grandma and Mom came by to do some shopping. First they bought cabbages and ice cream, then they bought lettuce and potato chips and a model helicopter and a doll's tea set. Mr. Lewis Burrows took the money and counted out the change, and his assistant handed things over the counter.

The shop stayed open all afternoon.

When it was time to go indoors, Mom made a notice and fixed it with a piece of string so that Alfie could hang it up outside the shop. On one side it said:

But when you turned it round it said:

"Even Mr. Lewis Burrows has to go to bed sometime, I expect," said Mom.

Fallen Giant

A big tree
lying down
is like a giant
with torn-out roots
instead of feet.
It's like a ship
sailing far out to sea,
or a house with many rooms.
It has places to hide
and swing on
and climb along.
A big tree
lying down
is a good place to play.
But you can never make it stand up again.
Not ever.

Alfie Goes Camping

One summer afternoon Mom hung a sheet over the clothesline and weighted it down with stones on either side. Alfie crawled inside. It made a good tent.

"I'm camping," Alfie called out. "This is my tent and nobody can come in here unless I say so!"

But Annie Rose was already coming in through the other end, uninvited.

Alfie went indoors and brought out some important things to put in his tent. He brought a coloring book and some crayons, a saucepan, his old blanket, and his knitted elephant. He spread a rug inside and some cushions to sit on.

"Real campers cook their food over a camp fire and eat it sitting on the ground," Alfie told Annie Rose. So they put some bits of grass into the saucepan and cooked them over a pretend fire.

After that they went inside the tent and lay down
on the cushions. Alfie pretended it was nighttime and
there was a forest all around full of wolves, snakes, and
snarling tigers.

Annie Rose was not quite sure whether she liked
this part of the game, and she soon trotted indoors to
find Mom.

Alfie was still in his tent when Dad came home from work. He brought out a mug of tea and drank it sitting by Alfie's camp fire.

Dad told Alfie that he had owned a real tent when he was a boy and had slept out in it all night.

"I'll look in the attic and see if it's still there," he promised. "And if it is, we might try it out next time we go to visit Grandma in the country."

Dad did find the tent. Alfie was very excited when
the time came to put it up in the field next to Grandma's
house. Everyone came out to watch. It was big enough
for two people to lie down in.

Annie Rose was too little to go camping, so it was going
to be just Alfie and Dad. They had brought proper foam
mattresses and sleeping bags with them from home.
"I hope it doesn't rain," said Dad.

Alfie could hardly wait until bedtime. He kept going in and out of the tent to check that everything was ready. He had put his blanket and elephant beside his sleeping bag. Dad had put a flashlight beside his.

At last bedtime came. Alfie had a wash and put on his pajamas and bathrobe just as usual. He wanted to cook his own supper over a camp fire, but Dad said that might be a bit difficult.

Instead they had supper in the kitchen, baked potatoes and baked beans. Grandma gave them some apples to take with them into the tent.

Then they set out. It was strange not to be going upstairs to bed but down the yard, through the gate, and into the field.

It was still light. Dad and Alfie sat down in front
of the tent with a blanket around them and ate their
apples. They watched the sun go down behind the trees.
They watched the sky change color. They saw the
birds swooping and calling to one another. They sat
there until it was quite dark and the stars came out,
one by one.

It was very mysterious to be outside at night under
the big sky, with rustling noises all around and the wind
blowing the branches about. But Alfie felt very safe
being there with Dad.

Just before it was time to settle down, Alfie jumped up, scampered off across the field, and did a little dance all by himself under the stars.

Then they climbed into their sleeping bags and Alfie cuddled up to his blanket with his elephant in beside him and went off to sleep.

When he woke up
it wasn't morning.
It was the middle of the night.
It was completely dark,
not like being in a bedroom
with the light shining in
from the landing, but
pitch-black all around.

Alfie put out his hand. He could feel Dad's back next
to him, humped up inside the sleeping bag. Alfie lay
very still and listened. He could hear noises outside,
strange creakings and flappings.

Inside the tent he could
hear Dad breathing. But
then Alfie realized that he
could hear something else
breathing, too. And that
something was
outside the tent!

Alfie sat up.
He didn't scream.
He didn't even cry.
He just leaned over
and wrapped his arms
around Dad's neck and
squeezed very tightly
indeed. Then, of course,
Dad woke up, too.

Now the breathing thing was just near their heads. It was a very snorty, snuffly sort of breathing. They could hear it moving, too. It was trampling about in the grass. Then it went round the tent to the zip opening, which Dad had left not quite done up, and started to push against it.

Alfie was quite sure that something huge and horrible was coming to eat them up. He began to scream and scream.

"It's okay, Alfie," said Dad. He felt for his flashlight and switched it on.

They saw a big pink nose coming through the tent flap. It had very large wet nostrils.

"It's a pig!" said Dad. And he bravely got out of his sleeping bag and gave the nose a big push.

Alfie stopped screaming. He and Dad crawled out of the tent. It did not seem quite so dark outside. The pig moved a short distance away and stood there watching them.

"I didn't know Jim Gatting had put his pig in this field," grumbled Dad sleepily. He tried to make the pig go away, but it wouldn't.

After a while they tried to go back to sleep in the tent, but the pig kept trying to join them.

In the end there was nothing for it but to take the tent down. They collected up all their things and carried them back into Grandma's yard. It took several journeys to and fro. The pig followed closely behind them.

When Dad finally closed the gate on the pig, it stuck its snout through the bars and watched them.

Dad told Alfie that they couldn't very well wake up everybody in the house at that time of night, so they had better put up the tent again in the yard. Alfie thought that was a very good idea.

At last they got the tent back up and crawled into it, and the pig got tired of watching and wandered off down the field.

Alfie and Dad dozed until it was nearly light.

When Alfie woke again, Dad was still fast asleep. Alfie crept quietly out of his sleeping bag and stood in the wet grass in his bare feet. The curtains of Grandma's house were still tightly drawn. But the sun was up and the birds were making a great noise.

Alfie felt very special to be the only person awake and out-of-doors that sunny morning. And he made up his mind to ask Dad if they could go camping again that very night.

Moon

When it's dark
Alfie likes to see the moon
up above the houses.
Sometimes it has a round face,
glittering bright,
making sharp black shadows race across the garden.
Sometimes it's a pale, thin slice of moon,
lying on its back
and riding the clouds.

The sun is always round,
so bright that you have to screw up your eyes to look
and shut them up again quickly.
Even then you can still see it,
floating like a penny across your eyelids.
But the moon is a silver light,
always changing,
every night a little bit different.
Magic moon.

Lost Sheep

Grandma's house had a long yard at the back and a small yard in front with a gate which led into the lane. If you walked one way, you came to the road and more houses. If you walked the other way, up the hill, there were trees, hedges, and fields. In the fields lived cows and sheep.

The cows went up to the farm twice a day to be milked. They walked follow-the-leader in a long straggly line. The rest of the time they stayed in the field, munching. Alfie liked the slow way they lowered their necks and pulled up great mouthfuls of grass. When he and Grandma passed by, the cows came to the fence and stood in a row, looking over curiously with big brown eyes, swishing their tails and breathing hard through their noses.

Cows were very nice. But best of all Alfie liked sheep. Sheep were his favorite animals. He especially liked the ones with black faces, and bony black legs sticking out below their large woolly bodies.

The field where the sheep lived was farther up the hill. When Alfie climbed the gate to say hello to them, they trotted away and stood baaing at him from a safe distance.

One day when Alfie and Grandma were out for a walk together, they saw a black-faced sheep standing in the middle of the lane all by herself. She was baaing very loudly at the other sheep, and they were baaing back from behind the fence.

"Oh dear, that sheep's gotten out somehow," said Grandma. "She must have gotten through a hole in the fence."

"I think she wants to get back to the others," said Alfie.

As they came nearer to the sheep, she ran on up the lane. Every so often she stopped and looked through the fence as though she was trying to find a way back. But when Alfie and Grandma came close to try to help her, she shook her woolly tail at them and ran on. She wouldn't let them catch up with her.

The more they hurried behind her, the faster she ran. Soon she had left her own field behind and reached another field, full of cows. They put their heads over the fence and mooed at her. The poor sheep baaed back. She looked very puzzled and lost.

Then she ran on again. She ran to the top of the hill where big trees grew on either side of the lane.

"We'd better not follow her any farther," said Grandma. "She'll just run on and on, and we'll never be able to catch her."

Alfie and Grandma stood still and wondered what
to do. The sheep stopped, too. She stood a good distance
away, but she turned her head to look at them and
baaed anxiously.

"Let's just stand here for a while and see what
happens," said Grandma.

Alfie and Grandma stood together hand in hand on the grassy bank. Alfie found it very hard to stand still for long, but he pretended he was a tree growing by the fence and that made it easier.

For a long while the sheep just stood and stared at them. Then she started to trot back down the lane toward them. Grandma and Alfie squeezed each other's hands tightly. They stood as still as still. The sheep came nearer and paused. Then she stepped daintily past them, holding up her head proudly and pretending not to notice them at all.

Alfie and Grandma stood and watched her large
woolly back hurrying away round the bend in the lane.
They waited awhile before they started to walk home.
When they reached the field where the sheep lived, the
lane was empty.

"Our sheep must have found her own way back into
the field with the others," said Grandma.

Alfie climbed the gate to look. The sheep turned their heads to look back at him. It was very hard to tell which was the one who had gotten lost.

"Well done, black-faced sheep!" shouted Alfie, waving. And all the sheep baaed back.

Creepy Crawly World

Lift up a stone and you can see
a creepy crawly world.
You can watch the creepy crawlies hurrying about,
busily moving on many legs,
with strangely shaped bodies
and feelers –
for feeling their way along.

In a creepy crawly world,
a tiny piece of twig is like a giant log
that has to be pushed,
or pulled,
or climbed over,
or patiently gone round.
Creepy crawlies don't mind how long it takes
to get where they are going.
But why they want to get there,
nobody knows.

Bonting

One fine summer morning Alfie went out into the backyard to look around, and he found a stone. It was a
specially nice sort of gray stone, worn very smooth all
over with white streaks in it. It was rounded on one side
and flattish on the other, and it fitted well into the palm
of Alfie's hand.

Alfie turned the stone over and over and passed it
from one hand to the other. Then he put it into the
pocket of his shorts.

He kept it there all
day. Whenever he put his
hand into his pocket, it felt
comforting. By the end of
the day Alfie had decided
that the stone had become
a real friend, and he called
it Bonting.

Alfie liked Bonting a lot. He liked him almost as
much as his blanket and his knitted elephant. Alfie's
elephant was old, nearly as old as Alfie. But Mom said
that Bonting was a lot older than that. He was very old,
perhaps thousands and thousands of years. Alfie didn't
know anybody as old as that, so it made Bonting even
more special.

Mom gave Alfie a box lined with cotton batting for Bonting to sleep in. He put it on the nightstand next to his bed.

Alfie's elephant wore a scarf and a hat to match, which Grandma had knitted for him. He looked very smart in them.

Alfie asked Mom if she would please make some clothes for Bonting, too. Mom said that Bonting looked as though he might be a difficult shape to fit, but she would do her best. She and Alfie looked into the basket where Mom kept her snippets of stuff, and Alfie chose a bit with green-and-black stripes.

Then Mom made a hat for Bonting and a scarf which tied round his middle. There was a bit of stuff left over, so she made him a bathing suit as well.

The bathing suit was a good idea, because the weather was getting hot.

Alfie and Annie Rose played in the backyard, splashing about in the paddling pool and sailing their toy boats. Bonting didn't float in the water. He sank straight down to the bottom and stayed there.

When Dad came home, he said that if the weather stayed hot and sunny they would get up very early and drive to the seaside.

Alfie was very excited. He had seen the sea before, but that was a very long time ago and he couldn't quite remember what it looked like.

Mom got the picnic ready, and they packed up the towels and sun hats and bathing suits and Alfie's armbands for swimming and the buckets and spades and put them in the car. Bonting came too, of course, inside Alfie's pocket.

It was a long drive. Inside, the car got hotter and hotter. Annie Rose went to sleep. Alfie looked out of the window hoping to see the sea, but all he could see were cars, trucks, and motorcycles.

At last they arrived! The sea was huge, almost as big as the sky. It stretched away and away, full of sparkling light. Far out there were big waves. Where the sea met the beach, it broke into little waves.

They arched over one another, running up the sand and then out again, sucking seaweed and pebbles with them. Alfie stood still and looked. He just couldn't stop looking.

The first thing they did was change into their bathing
suits and run into the waves.

Then they raced each other up the beach and ate their picnic. Bonting had a little piece of Alfie's sandwich.

After lunch Alfie gave Bonting a swim in a pool and put him carefully to dry in the sun.

Then Alfie dug a sand castle (Dad and Annie Rose helped). And they threw a ball about.

They collected shells and bits of frilly seaweed, and looked at little fish and crabs hiding in pools, under the rocks.

At last, when the tide had gone out, leaving miles and miles of shining sand, and Alfie's shadow was getting longer and longer, Mom and Dad started to pack up the towels and the picnic things and get ready to go home. Alfie and Annie Rose fetched their spades and buckets full of all the special things they had collected.

Then Alfie felt in his pocket to check that Bonting was still there. But he wasn't! He remembered that he had put him out to dry after his swim. He ran anxiously to the place where he had left him.

But Bonting was nowhere to be seen! Alfie looked all around. There were stones everywhere, hundreds and hundreds of them, but not one was wearing a green-and-black-striped bathing suit. Alfie began to be very upset.

Of course Mom and Dad started to look for Bonting.
They hunted up and down the beach, turning over
pebbles with their feet and peering into rock pools.
Annie Rose hunted, too. But they couldn't find him.
After a long search, Dad said that it was getting so late
– way past Alfie's and Annie Rose's bedtime – that they
really had to start for home.

"But we can't leave Bonting behind!" wailed Alfie.
"He'll be all lonely on the beach at night!"

Dad put his arm round
Alfie and explained that
Bonting wouldn't be
lonely because he would
have so many other stones
to keep him company. So
he wouldn't mind at all.

All the same, Alfie cried all the way to the parking lot and part of the way home in the car. In the end he was so tired that he fell asleep, and so did Annie Rose.

It was very late when they arrived home. They hardly woke up when Mom and Dad carried them into the house and put them to bed.

In the morning, the first thing Alfie saw when he woke up was Bonting's empty box, and he felt sad.

After breakfast he and Annie Rose went into the backyard where Mom was hanging out the bathing suits and towels.

Their buckets and spades were by the back door. Alfie began to sort through his bucket. He had collected some lovely shells and some nice stones. He lined them up in a row on the doorstep. But none of them was quite as nice as Bonting.

Annie Rose's bucket was full of seaweed and muddy water. She picked it up and tipped out the whole lot onto the ground. There was a strong smell of seaside.

Then Alfie and Annie Rose looked into the bottom of Annie Rose's bucket, and what do you think they saw?

It was Bonting! His green-and-black bathing suit was all sopping wet and covered with mud. Alfie was *very* pleased to see him.

"Bonting will have to have a new bathing suit," he told Mom.

"His next one had better be bright red," said Mom. "Then he'll be easier to find if you decide to take him for another swim."

Sea Sound

The sea, the sea!
Can you hear the sea?
Big waves like green marble,
rocking and swelling far away from land;
small splashy waves
coming in one upon another,
in long curving lines along the shore,
rushing in among the rocks,
filling up the pools
where crabs and little fishes hide.

Even when summer days are over,
and Alfie is snuggled down in his warm bed,
he sometimes puts a seashell to his ear
to hear the sea.

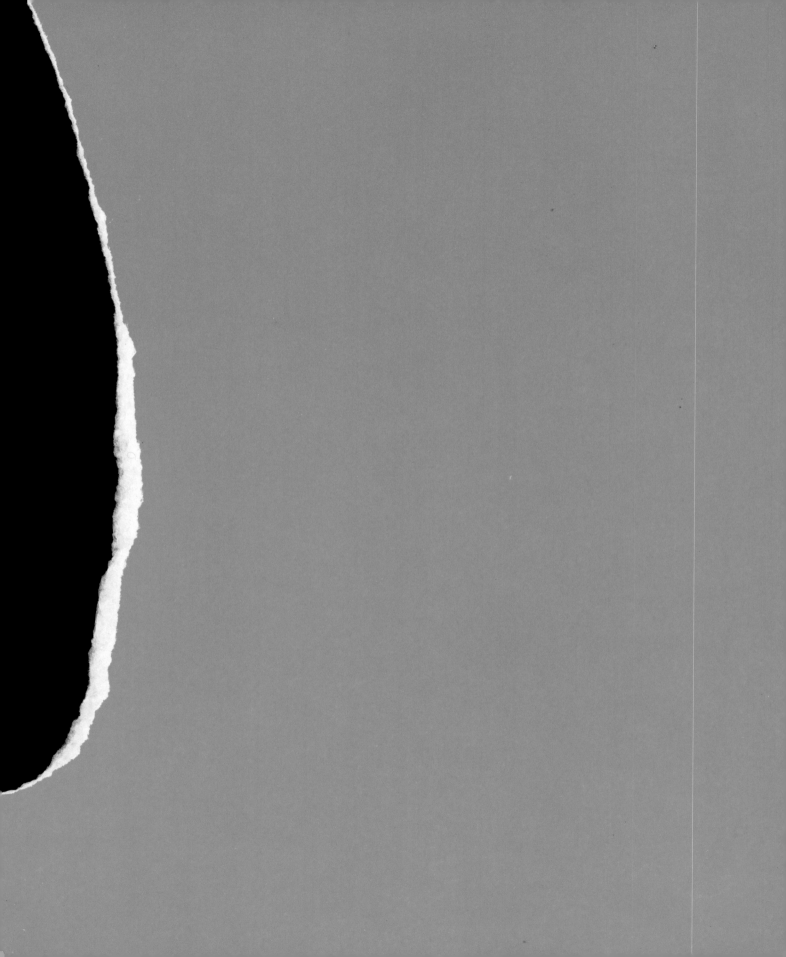